Stanley, the Stalwart Dragon

by Trisha Sugarek

Baker's Plays
7611 Sunset Blvd.
Los Angeles, CA 90042
bakersplays.com

CHARACTERS

STARE – The rhetorical owl.

STANLEY – The dragon is a gentle soul, different from everyone at home. He wears glasses, is soft spoken and, for the life of him, can't breathe fire.

DONALD – The good and kind faerie. He and Emma are best friends.

PERSNICKETY – A Lady Bug. She is Stanley's sidekick. She is fussy about everything.

CHEETS – A mischievous elf. He is never still or quiet. He jumps, runs, hops, skips around the stage. He has bigger ears, feet and brain than Donald and the other faeries. Not gender specific.

EMMA – An earthling girl. She is the Queen's favorite since she rescued the Unicorn from a century old curse.

CLEO – Queen of the faeries, she reins over the forest and she and her handmaidens care for the all the faeries and woodland creatures.

SCARLET
YELLOW
ORANGE
BLUE
PURPLE
GREEN – Young handmaidens to the Queen. They are dressed in their respective colors. Long flowing gowns, reminiscent of Medieval times. Their hands, feet and faces and wings are the same color as their gowns and their names.

THOMAS – A big sea Turtle. He is plodding, slow, in his movements and speech. He only speaks in nautical terms. *(See glossary)*

CITY SLICK THE THIRD – A Raven who is a wise guy, a slick operator, always got a deal going. He wants to lure Stanley to the bright lights of the Circus and sell him.

FRECKLES – The Circus owner and clown.

Various faeries and small creatures of the forest. Rabbits, skunks, squirrels, fawns, to include children of all ages in non-speaking parts. Some can be double cast as circus people and animals for Act II. The ballerina is optional.

PRODUCTION NOTES

STANLEY never breathes fire. The best he can do is blow bubbles and should have the capacity to do so throughout the performance. He should be as large as he can be so that at first he frightens everyone. He wears horn rimmed glasses. He burps bubbles when he is emotional.

SLICK, the Raven should always speak in tones like a circus barker, a dealer wheeler, a wise guy. He lives for the next deal. In Act I, he is dressed in black except a diamond patterned vest in black and white. He wears a black derby hat. In Act II his vest is bright yellow. He wears a yellow feather in his hat.

QUEEN CLEO speaks in the royal 'we'. This is not a grammatical error.

The toad stool that **STANLEY** sits on should be a little larger than the others, but still small enough to look ludicrous when he sits on it.

PERSNICKETY should straighten, trim, organize, clean, the entire time on stage. She could carry a very small whist broom and dust pan on her belt.

FRECKLES, the clown is in full clown make up with a down turned mouth and large freckles. He wears a large key on a chain.

Act II, Sc.2 and 3: There is a set change to the Circus. This must be simple enough to strike between scenes. There should be a sound track of the circus audience. Scene 3 opens with Circus Theme music.

Act II: The back stage of the circus can be suggestive. A canvas tarp can be laid on the forest floor. A large colorful drum; the type that the circus master stands on. Some ropes are hanging from above to suggest a tent and the trapeze. The chain around **STANLEY**'s ankle should be very large. During the circus scenes **STARE** exits the stage.

Act II, Sc.4: The **BALLERINA** is optional.

Act II, Sc. 9: When **STANLEY** and **PERSNICKETY** fly away, the actors should follow their flight with their heads and bodies as **STANLEY** makes the large circle and heads in the right direction. If budget allows **STANLEY** could actually 'fly' away.

Any more questions? Please contact the playwright through
her web site:
www.writeratplay.com

To children everywhere…
You are my inspiration.

ACT I

Scene One

*(**AT RISE**: A lush, deep, enchanted forest. It is quiet and still with the exception of a hooting owl and occasional bird song.)*

*(There is thrashing in the underbrush and **STANLEY** enters from between the trees. His tie is crooked, his glasses askew and he has leaves and twigs all over him. He acts very bold at first.)*

STANLEY. I'll show them! They can't treat me like this.

STARE. Whooo??

*(**STANLEY**, losing his bravado quickly, looks around the scary forest. He sits down on a small toad stool and squishes it flat. Sighing he rises and sits on a larger one.)*

STANLEY. Oh, dear, oh dear! I fear I am lost.

STARE. Who?

STANLEY. Me.

STARE. Who?

*(**STANLEY** rises and takes a brave stance.)*

STANLEY. Me. Me! *(sees **STARE**)* Who are you? Friend or foe?

STARE. Who.

STANLEY. Don't you know any other question? I have one for *you;* where am I?

STARE. Who?

STANLEY. Well, Who, if you intend me harm, think again. I am a very fearsome dragon.

STARE. Who?

STANLEY. Me! That's who, Who! Friend or foe?

STARE. Who?

STANLEY. I know your name, but are you friend or…

   *(***DONALD*** enters.)*

DONALD. Hello. Can I help?

STANLEY. *(He whirls around at* **DONALD**'s *voice.)* Don't come any closer! I am a fire breathing dragon.

   (Out of the forest rushes **PERSNICKETY**, **STANLEY**'s *friend and sidekick.)*

PERSNICKETY. There you are, you bad dragon! I thought I told you to wait for me….

   *(***PERSNICKETY*** sees ***DONALD*** and stands in front of* **STANLEY** *to defend him.)*

PERSNICKETY. Please, Sir. Do not hurt him. He really is a very nice dragon.

   *(***DONALD**, with a courtly bow.)*

DONALD. I mean you no harm, Mr. Dragon. My name is Donald and I'm very pleased to meet you.

STANLEY. You are?

PERSNICKETY. You are?

STARE. Who?

DONALD. Quiet.

STARE. Who?

STANLEY. Who?

PERSNICKETY. Excuse me?

DONALD. I was talking to Stare, the owl.

   *(***STANLEY*** swings his head to* **STARE** *and glares at him.)*

STANLEY. He told me his name is 'Who'.

STARE. *(indignant)* Who?

DONALD. *(laughing)* No…that's what he *asks*. He asks far too many questions and they are always the same. But, his name is Stare.

STANLEY. Well, it wasn't very nice of him to lie to me.

STARE. Who?!

STANLEY. You!

PERSNICKETY. What beautiful manners you have, Donald. My name is Persnickety and this messy dragon is Stanley the Stalwart.

(**PERSNICKETY** *crosses to* **STANLEY** *and starts picking off leaves and twigs, straightening his tie.*)

PERSNICKETY. Really, Stanley. You're in no state to meet new people. Just look at you! I leave you alone for two seconds and you get all dirty.

STANLEY. Sorry, Nickety.

PERSNICKETY. *(referring to nickname)* What did I tell you?

DONALD. I am certain it was a misunderstanding about Stare's name. He is a nice owl and generally very truthful. *(beat)* May I call you Stanley?

STANLEY. Yes. But don't call her 'Nickety'. She gets mad.

(*Laughing,* **DONALD** *approaches* **STANLEY** *and holds out his hand to shake.*)

DONALD. How do you do, Stanley. *(shakes her hand)* Persnickety.

STANLEY. Not so well, Donald. I fear that we are lost. Where is this exactly and…*what* are you?

PERSNICKETY. Stanley, what a rude question!

DONALD. No, no, not at all. I am a faerie. You are in our forest. Well, really it's Emma's forest since Hazard gave it to her. Cleo, the Queen of the Faeries rules over us all, as we are an enchanted forest. I am Emma's friend. Cheets, who is an elf, will take some getting used to. Hazard used to be a bad man but he married Emma's mother so…. *(takes a big breath to continue)*

STANLEY. Wait! Wait. You're making my head hurt. Can we go slower?

DONALD. Of course. I'm sorry. You say you and Persnickety are lost, Stanley? Where do you live?

(**CHEETS** *runs on and skitters to a stop in front of* **DONALD.***)*

CHEETS. Okay! Who's got the dragon's breath? *(runs around)* Ewwww! Dragon Breath! Dragon Breath!

DONALD. Cheets! Stop that at once! Stanley does not have bad breath.

CHEETS. *(spies* **STANLEY***)* Whoa!! *What is it?*

DONALD. Where are your manners? That's not a 'it'. That's a 'he'. This is Stanley.

CHEETS. What is '*he*'?

DONALD. Stanley's a dragon.

CHEETS. I *knew* I smelled dragon breath!

DONALD. Cheets, will you stop being so rude? Stanley is my new friend and he does not have dragon's breath.

(Hands on hips, **CHEETS** *walks around* **STANLEY** *staying a safe distance from him.)*

CHEETS. So, what's he doing here in our forest? Is he lost? Is he on the lamb? Did he burn down a village? Is he going to burn down our forest?

(runs around more agitated)

CHEETS. Fire! Fire! Get the Queen. Sound the alarm! FIRE!

STARE. Who?

DONALD. Cheets! Stop yelling. I am certain that Stanley is a good dragon and isn't going to set fire to anything. *(Beat. Worried:)* Would you, Stanley?

PERSNICKETY. Certainly not!

STANLEY. No, Donald. You see, that's why…

(Trumpets sound, music plays, bells ring. **QUEEN CLEO** *and her* **ENTOURAGE** *enter.* **EMMA** *is with the* **QUEEN***.* **CHEETS** *runs around frantically.)*

CHEETS. The Queen!! The Queen cometh! Long live the Queen.

(runs to **STANLEY** *and around him, always keeping a safe distance)*

Hey, Dragon Breath, better run away. The Queen is coming.

STARE. Who?

DONALD. Cheets!

> (**CHEETS** *makes an awkward, courtly bow to* **QUEEN CLEO**. *The Queen's* **HANDMAIDENS** *cower in a fearful group when they see the dragon.*)

CHEETS. Your Majesty. Wait 'till you see what I've got! You are going to be so surprised. I captured it. I was very brave. *(pointing to* **STANLEY***)* LOOK!!

> (**QUEEN CLEO** *acknowledges* **STANLEY** *but addresses* **DONALD**.*)*

QUEEN CLEO. Sir Donald. We are pleased to see you. Who is this fine, young dragon that visits our forest?

CHEETS. I *told* you, your Majesty! I was very brave, like a knight at your court… It's a dragon, he breathes fire, I saw it with my very own eyes and I captured him.

PERSNICKETY. He did not!

STANLEY. I didn't breathe any fire.

QUEEN CLEO. *(sternly)* Cheets, do you need a time out?

> (**CHEETS** *skids to a stop.)*

CHEETS. No, Ma'am. Cheets will be good. See? Cheets will sit down over here.

> *(He sits.)*

QUEEN CLEO. Sir Donald?

STARE. Who?

QUEEN CLEO. Oh, Stare, we did not see you. How do you fare?

> (**STARE** *ruffles his feathers with delight at being noticed by his* **QUEEN**.*)*

STARE. Whoooo.

DONALD. My Queen, may I present my new friends, Stanley and Persnickety? They seem to be lost. Stanley, this is the Queen of the faeries, Queen Cleo. Her majesty rules over all.

(**STANLEY** *gives a surprisingly graceful bow given his size.* **PERSNICKETY** *gives a perfect curtsey.*)

STANLEY. Your Majesty.

PERSNICKETY. Charmed, Your Grace.

DONALD. These lovely ladies are her ladies in waiting. And, this is my dear friend, Emma.

STANLEY. Ladies.

(*The* **HANDMAIDENS** *shake with fear.*)

PERSNICKETY. Oh, Stanley, look at their lovely gowns. They look like a field of flowers. And, Emma. What a charming child.

STANLEY. Miss Emma.

(**EMMA** *rushes over, without any fear, and hugs* **STANLEY.**)

EMMA. Stanley, you are so beautiful. Are you a real dragon? Do you truly spit fire? *(laughs)* We will never need a match again!

(**STANLEY** *blushes.*)

QUEEN CLEO. Mr. Dragon…

STANLEY. Excuse me, your Majesty, but my name is Stanley the Stalwart. Please do me the honour of calling me 'Stanley'.

QUEEN CLEO. Well, Stanley, your mother must be very proud of her '*stalwart*' son.

STANLEY. That's the problem, your Majesty. She isn't. I didn't turn out very well.

PERSNICKETY. That's not the case at all!

DONALD. Stanley, I'm sure that's not true.

STANLEY. Sadly, it is. I am a great disappointment to my Mother…and Father.

(**CLEO** *turns to her ladies.*)

QUEEN CLEO. Ladies…our chair… *(notices that they are afraid)* For heavens sakes, there is nothing to fear here. Scarlet, Blue, Orange, our chair.

(The **HANDMAIDENS** *hurry to bring a large flower throne over to the* **QUEEN***. She sits.* **EMMA** *sits at her knee. The* **HANDMAIDENS** *gather around the* **QUEEN***.* **CHEETS** *jumps up and runs around the* **QUEEN** *and the stage.)*

*(***PERSNICKETY** *crosses to the* **QUEEN** *and fusses with the folds of her gown.* **PERSNICKETY** *straightens* **EMMA***'s hair bow.)*

STANLEY. Persnickety, stop fussing. Forgive her, your Majesty, Nickety can't bear for things to be messy or less than perfect.

PERSNICKETY. I apologize, Your Grace, if I offend.

EMMA. I think it's cute.

STARE. Who?

QUEEN CLEO. No offense taken, Stanley. Now that we are all settled, will you tell us what brings you here to our forest?

*(***CHEETS** *runs across the stage, shouting.)*

CHEETS. A story! A story! Hurry, everyone, there's going to be a story!

(As everyone is settling into their seats, the **WOODLAND CREATURES** *begin to cautiously emerge from the forest. Faeries flit about and settle.)*

QUEEN CLEO. Donald, Stanley, please be seated.

*(***DONALD** *begins to sit and* **CHEETS** *runs over and takes the toad stool where* **DONALD** *was going to sit.)*

EMMA. Oh, yes please, Stanley, tell us your tale.

*(***THOMAS***, the sea turtle enters the clearing in his plodding manner. He crosses to the* **QUEEN** *and* **EMMA***.)*

THOMAS. Shiver me timbers, Your Grace. What a motley crew!

EMMA. Hello, Thomas! Where have you been?

QUEEN CLEO. Thomas, we have missed you. May we introduce our new friends to you?

(*STANLEY rises from his stool.* **THOMAS** *and* **STANLEY** *eye each other and don't like what they see.*)

THOMAS. What is *that*? In all my travels I've never seen any-thing…

STANLEY. What is a 'Thomas'? And what's that he's wear-ing?

(*Everyone laughs at their reaction to one another.*)

THOMAS. Looks like a sea monster I spied once off the coast of Africa.

STANLEY. He looks like my mother's pie plate set up-side-down.

THOMAS. I do not!

STANLEY. I am not!

PERSNICKETY. He does not!

CHEETS. Fight! Fight!

QUEEN CLEO. Please, please, one at a time. Cheets, sit down. There will be no fighting.

THOMAS. Batten the hatches, there's a sea monster amongst us!

STANLEY. I. AM. NOT. A. SEA. MONSTER.

(*STANLEY is upset and rears back his head and blows… bubbles all over* **THOMAS**.)

EMMA. (*Rising, she crosses to* **STANLEY** *and takes his hand.*) Dear Stanley, don't be upset. Of course you're not a sea monster. Thomas didn't mean to insult you and hurt your feelings. Did you, Thomas?

THOMAS. No, I guess not.

EMMA. Say you're sorry, Thomas.

THOMAS. But, Miss Emma, there's a strange tide that's runnin' today…

(**EMMA** *waits.* **THOMAS** *pauses.*)

…Sor–rey!

EMMA. Stanley?

STANLEY. Sorry for the pie plate remark.

PERSNICKETY. Very well done, Emma.

EMMA. Wonderful! Now we're all friends. Just because we're different from each other, doesn't mean we can't be friends. After all, I'm an earthling and you are all enchanted creatures and faeries *(Smiles at* **CHEETS.***)* *and elves* and yet we're all the best of friends, aren't we? Remember when I was crippled with my bad leg…you didn't call me names or laugh because I walked funny. You were all very kind to me. *(beat)* Stanley, Thomas is a sea turtle. He is a very famous Captain and has sailed the world.

(**THOMAS** *puffs up with pride and* **STANLEY** *stares at him in fascination.)*

EMMA. And Thomas, Stanley is a…

(**CHEETS** *jumps up and runs to* **EMMA,** *nearly knocking her down.)*

CHEETS. Let me! Let me tell, Emma. I found him!

DONALD. You didn't!

CHEETS. Did too.

STARE. *(indignant because he saw* **STANLEY** *first)* WHO!!

PERSNICKETY. *(indicating* **CHEETS***)* Who and what *is this?*

DONALD. Oh no, here we go…

EMMA. Cheets is a…

CHEETS. Cheets is an Elf! I am *not* a faerie. Cheets has bigger feet, the better to run with, Cheets has bigger ears, the better to hear with, Cheets has a bigger brain…the better to think with.

THOMAS. Good grief! There's a hot wind a'blowin'.

STARE. Who?

PERSNICKETY. You're a very odd little thing.

EMMA. Dear Miss Persnickety, we're all special each in our own way, don't you think?

CHEETS. Cheets will now tell the story of how he captured the fire breathing dragon.

(**CHEETS** *begins speaking rapidly, moving all the time and gesturing.)*

CHEETS. Donald and I were alone here in the forest…

STARE. *(indignant)* Who?

CHEETS. …and I said to Donald, 'I smell dragon breath' and Donald said that he didn't smell anything. Then the bushes and trees started to shake and tremble and Donald was afraid. But I wasn't. Then I said, in a loud voice, 'Come out and show yourself!' And this dragon burst from the forest, breathing fire and barely missed us and I captured him and then the Queen came and now he's subdued but watch out…he could spew fire at any moment…

QUEEN CLEO. Cheets, what have I told you about telling fibs?

DONALD. What a ridiculous tall tale, Cheets.

CHEETS. Most of it's true. Show 'em, Stanley. Set fire to that bush over there.

> (**STANLEY,** *not wanting to disappoint, rears his head back and blows bubbles toward the bush. Everyone laughs except for the* **QUEEN, DONALD,** *and* **EMMA.** **STANLEY** *hangs his head in shame.)*

PERSNICKETY. Oh, dear.

EMMA. Stanley, they aren't laughing *at* you. They are laughing because the bubbles make them so happy. They're such pretty bubbles, like a rainbow. Isn't that right, everyone?

(Ashamed, everyone eagerly agrees.)

THOMAS. He certainly is sensitive for a sea mons…*dragon.* He wouldn't last a day on one of my ships! I remember when we rounded the Cape of Good Hope, with Africa on our starboard…it was a stormy night and a sea monster emerged out of the black waters…

QUEEN CLEO. Thomas. We would love to hear that story…. but perhaps another time. Stanley was about to tell us how he ended up here in our forest so far from his home. *(She turns to* **STANLEY.***)* Stanley, now that we are all gathered, would you favor us with your tale?

PERSNICKETY. It's a good one, Your Grace!

(**STANLEY** *sits again and* **EMMA** *sits next to him.*)

STANLEY. I grew up far, far from here on an island called Clymene. My dragon clan are direct descendants of the mystical dragon, Ladon, who guarded Hesperides' garden. In the garden there was a tree that bore golden apples. Many eons ago Hercules killed Ladon so he could possess the golden apples. So my ancestors fled to our island and we have lived there ever since. My ancestors were all fierce dragons. My grandfather could burn down a whole village with one exhale. *(Everyone 'Oohs and Ahs'.)* My parents expected great things from me.

STARE. Who?

STANLEY. My parents…

STARE. Who?

(**STANLEY** *looks perplexed.*)

EMMA. Don't answer him Stanley. If you do we'll be here all day. Now, tell us why you think you didn't turn out well.

STANLEY. *(ashamed)* I'm not fierce. I can't stand the thought of burning someone's village down. I don't want to defeat the black knights. I… *(Beat. Sighs.)* I…I can't breathe fire. Not a spurt, not even a puff of smoke.

EMMA. Oh! Poor, dear Stanley.

CHEETS. *(Jumps up. Runs around.)* Didn't Cheets say? He's got dragon breath. Dragon Breath! Dragon Breath!

QUEEN CLEO. Cheets! This is your warning.

(**CHEETS** *ignores the* **QUEEN.**)

CHEETS. I told Donald I smelled dragon's breat…

(**CLEO** *snaps her fingers and* **CHEETS** *freezes into a 'time out.'*)

QUEEN CLEO. Finally! Some peace and quiet.

DONALD. Go on, dear friend. What happened next?

STANLEY. When I was old enough, I went to dragon school. I got good grades except in Dragon Studies. We had fire breathing classes. I was very bad at it. My parents and the teachers thought the problem might be that I couldn't *see* the target so they got me glasses. I did need eye glasses, I can see ever so much better now. But it didn't cure my lack of…what was it my Dad called it?… 'the fire in my belly'. The other young dragons could light up anything. *Everything* was bursting into flames. But not me. I was a dud, a fizzle, a flop, a washout. My classmates called me names; Silly Stan, Simple Stalwart, Four eyes Stalwart, Sappy Stanley. I would get so angry I would take a deep breath…

(**STANLEY** *takes a deep breath and rears back his head as if to spew fire. Everyone ducks in fear.*)

PERSNICKETY. Don't worry….he can't…

STANLEY. …and try my best to toast 'em. But all I got was this…

(**STANLEY** *demonstrates and ends up by spewing bubbles over everyone.*)

THOMAS. (*under his breath*) Humph! Some sea monster.

(**CHEETS** *is squirming and shaking.*)

QUEEN CLEO. Cheets, are you going to behave?

(**CHEETS** *squirms in the affirmative.* **CLEO** *snaps her fingers.*)

Very well. Go and sit down and be quiet while Stanley finishes his story.

STARE. Who?

STANLEY. Me.

QUEEN CLEO. Stanley.

DONALD. Stare, quiet.

EMMA. Hush, Stare.

THOMAS. It's a high tide that's runnin' this day. A taller tale I've yet to hear.

QUEEN CLEO. Please continue, Stanley.

STANLEY. You see, I'm not stalwart at all. I am a great disappointment to my parents…especially my Father. He wanted me to be a fierce, fire breathing, warrior like my father and his father before him.

*(***CHEETS*** *starts to react but* **CLEO** *gives him a look and he subsides.)*

STANLEY. And so I. RAN. AWAY.

*(In her agitation, **PERSNICKETY** begins to sweep up.)*

PERSNICKETY. I told him not to. Bad idea, I said. Bad bad idea.

EMMA. Oh, Stanley.

*(She rises and crosses to **STANLEY**. She takes his hand.)*

Running away is never, *never* the answer, Stanley. Running away from home can be very dangerous. And think how worried your Mother and Father will be.

STANLEY. And now I'm lost.

PERSNICKETY. And now we're lost…

Scene Two

(AT RISE: The next day. **THOMAS, DONALD, STARE, STANLEY, PERSNICKETY** *and assorted woodland creatures and faeries are talking, playing games and the faeries are dancing.)*

*(***STANLEY*** *is on his back and little* **WOODLAND CREATURES** *and some of the smaller* **FAERIES** *are tickling him.* **STANLEY** *is laughing uncontrollably. He burps bubbles.)*

STANLEY. Oh! Oh, stop! I'm so ticklish…

(They roll around, giggling and laughing. **CHEETS** *runs on.)*

CHEETS. Better hide Stanley. Slick is back in the forest and he's headed this way.

THOMAS. Stow the grog. A raven has perched on the mizzen mast. Batten down the hatches! You there, Swabbie, man the foresail.

DONALD. You'd better hide in the forest, Stan, until we see what Slick wants.

PERSNICKETY. Why do we have to hide? *(She sniffs.)* It's just some old crow.

DONALD. That 'old crow' is Slick. He'd sell your grandmother for a nickel.

STANLEY. Why would anyone want to buy my grandmother?

THOMAS. He's worse luck than having a lady aboard one of my ships.

STANLEY. I'm not afraid of a little *bird!* *(He burps a bubble or two.)*

PERSNICKETY. Yeah, we're not afraid.

DONALD. Better safe than sorry. Stanley, please go into the forest and wait until I call you.

CHEETS. Slick's not such a bad egg.

THOMAS. Stow yourself in the hold until this squall blows over.

PERSNICKETY. I'll stay here, Stanley, and come and get you when it's safe.

STANLEY. But, Nickety, I don't want to hide. It's humiliating.

DONALD. It's just for a little while, Stan. Please.

STANLEY. Okay, Donald, if you think it best.

> (**STANLEY** *goes into the forest.* **SLICK** *enters and crosses to center stage. He addresses the audience and speaks like a circus barker or game show host. He is dressed all in black except for a white and black diamond patterned vest. He wears a black derby hat and carries a cane with an ivory top.*)

SLICK. Slick's the name, sales is the game! Step right up, folks. You want it, I can get it! Faerie dust, snake oil, beetle toes, eye of the newt, bee pollen, moon beams, bat hair, magic potions from the far East…

SLICK. *(He does a little soft shoe dance.)* *IT'S SHOW TIME!*

SLICK. Come one, come all…tell me your fondest wish! *(He twirls his cane.)* Your wife's fat, I can make her thin. Your mother-in-law is an ogre, I can sweeten her up. *RAZZMATAZZ!* *(He pulls a little brown bottle from a pocket. He taps the side with his finger.)* Is your hair falling out, boys, I can make it grow. You want him to love you, girls, try my Doctor Slick's love potion. Cures hair loss, warts, lonely hearts and bad breath.

CHEETS. I know someone who could use that!

DONALD. Not now, Cheets.

> (**DONALD** *and* **CHEETS** *cross down to* **SLICK.**)

CHEETS. Hi, Slick. Where've you been? We haven't seen you for a long time. Guess what we…

DONALD. Not now. Remember *who* we don't know anything about.

CHEETS. Oh yeah, I forgot.

SLICK. Donald! My main man! What can your buddy, Slick, do you for? I just blew back into town… *(pauses, gesturing to the forest)* or in this case, the 'burbs'. You should come with me, Donald. See the city lights. You'd love it!

CHEETS. Oh, Boy! 'City lights'. Can I come too?

SLICK. Certainly! The more the merrier. The rubes in town would pay good money to see your ears, Cheets.

CHEETS. They would? What are 'rubes'?

DONALD. Thanks anyway, Slick. We're happy right here at home.

STARE. Who?

CHEETS. What're 'rubes'?

DONALD. Never mind, Cheets!

STARE. Who?

> (**SLICK** *struts over to* **STARE***'s tree.*)

SLICK. Well, well, well. If it isn't the wise old owl. Learned any new words recently?

STARE. Who?

> (*mimics* **STARE**)

SLICK. Who? Who? What a loser!

STARE. *(indignant)* Who!

> (**CHEETS** *runs around yelling.*)

CHEETS. Who? Who? Who?

DONALD. Quiet!

STARE. Who?

DONALD. Never mind, Stare. *(beat)* What do you want, Slick?

SLICK. Why, Donald, buddy, I'm hurt. Why do you think I want something?

THOMAS. A foul wind blows...

DONALD. Maybe because you never show your face in our forest unless you want something. What is it this time?

SLICK. *(covering his heart with his wing)* You do me a grave injustice, Donald. I just came by to see my old friends.

STARE. Who?

SLICK. Silence! You old bag of feathers!

> (**SLICK** *rubs his hands together and grins.*)

Now, Donald, I think we have a little business to conduct.

CHEETS. Ah-ha!

DONALD. I knew it!

(**PERSNICKETY** *steps out from under a low handing tree.*)

SLICK. Hello! Who do we have here? *(crosses to* **PERSNICK-ETY***)* How're you doing? Slick's the name, sales is the game.

PERSNICKETY. How do you do? My name is Persnickety. *(beat)* Oh, dear, you have a smudge on your vest.

(**PERSNICKETY** *takes out her handkerchief, wets it with her tongue and dabs at the smudge.* **SLICK** *slaps her hand away.*)

SLICK. Hey! Don't put your spit on my coat. It cost a bundle. I don't have a smudge. Get off!

THOMAS. Reef your sails, Persnickety, it's a choppy sea.

(**SLICK** *turns back to* **DONALD.***)*

SLICK. I heard a rumor, Donald. A little birdie, no pun intended, told me that you and your little forest friends have a new play mate. Tweetie twittered in my ear that you caught a dragon.

(Silence. No one speaks. **CHEETS** *is silent but ready to burst.* **DONALD** *makes a grab for him and misses and* **CHEETS** *runs, hops, tumbles across the stage.)*

CHEETS. I know, I know! Donald didn't catch him…I…

PERSNICKETY. Cheets, hush!

SLICK. You know something!

CHEETS. YES! YES!

DONALD. NO! Cheets, don't tell!

PERSNICKETY. Cheets! Be quiet!

STARE. Who?

CHEETS. Cheets did it! Cheets caught a dragon. Cheets is so brave!

(**DONALD** *puts his head in his hands and groans.*)

SLICK. Donald, you disappoint me. Why would you want to keep this secret from me? *(crying)* Whyyyyy? *(Beat. Greedily rubbing his hands together.)* Now, where is he? Or is it a 'she'?

PERSNICKETY. Don't Cheets....

DONALD. Cheets, you've said enough....

CHEETS. It's a him. A very big him. He's got dragon breath and *EVERYTHING!*

*(**STANLEY** stumbles out of the forest.)*

STANLEY. Donald, how much longer must I stay hidden? Is he gone? The chiggers are biting me. *(aggrieved)* I have very sensitive skin, you know.

*(**STANLEY** stops when he sees **SLICK**.)*

STANLEY. Hello.

*(**SLICK** in his very best salesmen manner crosses to him.)*

SLICK. Hello! Hello. How-de-do! Let me present myself. I am City Slick, the Third. But my friends call me 'Slick'. Yessiree, Slick's the name, sales is my game. And you are...?

STANLEY. Nice to meet you, Sir. My name is Stanley...Stanley, the Stalwart Dragon.

*(**SLICK** is beside himself. He looks around at everyone.)*

SLICK. Oh, I love it! 'Stanley, the Stalwart Dragon'. Don't you just love it? *And* he talks! Can you blow a little fire for me, Stanley? Not too much, just a little?

STANLEY. No, Sir. I don't think that's such a good idea.

PERSNICKETY. Stanley is not a parlor game, Mr. Slick.

SLICK. Oh, come on, Stan, just a little burst for your old buddy, Slick.

DONALD. Leave him alone, Slick.

SLICK. Stay out of this, Donald. *(to **STANLEY**)* How 'bout a few puffs, Stan?

*(**EMMA** enters. She is focused on **STANLEY** and does not see **SLICK** at all.))*

EMMA. Good morning, everyone.

(*She crosses to* **STANLEY** *and holds out her arms.*)

Are you ready for your next dance lesson, Stanley?

STANLEY. Yes, Miss Emma. I've been practicing the steps you showed me.

(*They begin to waltz;* **STANLEY** *is a little clumsy.*)

SLICK. Oh, this is too rich. A talking, *dancing*, fire breathing dragon. My clients are gonna love him.

PERSNICKETY. What's a 'client'?

STARE. Who?

(**EMMA** *sees* **SLICK** *and stops dancing with* **STANLEY.**)

EMMA. What's he doing here, Donald? I thought the Queen banished him after the last time.

THOMAS. Pirates! Fly every rag we've got. You there, Swab-bie, get aloft and raise the topsail. Freebooters aft on the starboard side.

(**SLICK** *slides over to* **EMMA.** *Tries, unsuccessfully, to kiss her hand.*)

SLICK. Now now, my dear, the Queen and I have our differences all straightened out.

EMMA. You stole our hummingbirds. Right off my Mother's porch.

SLICK. No, no, my dear girl. That was all a big misunderstanding.

PERSNICKETY. What's a client?

EMMA. Ha!

STARE. Who?

EMMA. And I'm not 'your dear girl'.

THOMAS. Send the hornswoggling Picaroon to Davy Jones' Locker!

PERSNICKETY. (*Things are getting out of hand and going too fast for* **PERSNICKETY.**) What's a 'client'? What's a 'picaroon'? What's a 'hornswoggle'? Who's 'Davy Jones'?

STARE. Who?

EMMA. A client is like a customer.

DONALD. Thomas, will you explain the rest of it to us?

THOMAS. Be happy to, Boatswain. Keep forgetting you're all a bunch of landlubbers. A 'Hornswoggler' is a cheat, a fraud. 'Picaroon' is a rascal…

SLICK. Hey! Watch the name calling.

THOMAS. ….and 'Davy Jones' locker' is the bottom of the sea.

(THOMAS plods off and exits.)

Throw 'em overboard.

SLICK. My goodness. *(in all innocence)* An unhappy customer. What'd I ever do to him? *(beat)* Well, never mind.

(SLICK turns and crosses to STANLEY.)

Stanley, what say we talk a little business?

STANLEY. Huh?

STARE. Who?

DONALD. Slick…

SLICK. Stay out of this, Donald. Stan, my man, how do you feel about the circus?

PERSNICKETY. What's a circus?

STANLEY. A what?

(SLICK blusters.)

SLICK. 'What's a circus', you ask?! Are you kidding? The circus is the best place in the world. Ah! The big top! The smell of the sawdust! The elephants! The tigers! The trapeze! The freaks… *(coughs to cover his mistake)* …The *specialty acts* is what I meant to say. The pretty ladies who ride bareback on the horses. Cotton candy, popcorn, Peanuts! *(in his best 'barker's voice)* Peanuts! Get your red, hot peanuts here!

CHEETS. I *love* cotton candy!

STANLEY. Gosh, Mr. Slick, the circus sounds exciting.

SLICK. Oh it is! And they would *love* you, kid.

STANLEY. Me? Really?

SLICK. Really! Of course we'd have to control the bubbles. And teach you to breathe some fire…but, those are small details, my boy. Don't sweat the small stuff. That's Slick's motto.

EMMA. Stanley, you should think about going home.

DONALD. Let's think this through, Stan.

PERSNICKETY. I don't like it!

STARE. Who?!

PERSNICKETY. Me! That's 'who'. And what's your 'client' got to do with my friend?

SLICK. I misspoke, dear Lady. I meant that the families; the mothers, fathers, and children, who come to the circus, would love Stan.

STANLEY. Sounds like fun, Nickety. You know how much I love kids.

PERSNICKETY. Slow down, Stanley. This all sounds too good to be true.

EMMA. I agree.

STANLEY. But…

SLICK. Better than good, little Lady, and completely true. Stanley will be a star!

(**SLICK** *holds up his hands as if seeing the marquee with Stanley's name in lights.*)

He'll be the 'headliner' in the circus. I can see it now, 'Stanley, the fire-breathing dragon.' Nothing but the best. Limos, five star hotels, fine foods…

(**SLICK** *gets out a little black notebook.*)

Make a note, what do dragons eat. Arrange for extra large bed and towels, fresh fruit in the room. You do eat fruit, don'cha Stan?

STANLEY. Wow! I love fruit!

PERSNICKETY. Stanley…

SLICK. *And,* you, my dear 'Nickety. You could be his manager! I'll put a word in for you.

PERSNICKETY. Don't call me 'Nickety'. *(turns to* **STANLEY***)* See what you've started!

(Trumpets blare. Music plays announcing the arrival of the Queen. **QUEEN CLEO** *and her entourage enter. All bow and curtsey.)*

STANLEY. Your Majesty! Guess what? I'm joining the circus! Mr. Slick says that they'll love me! I'll be a success, at last.

*(***CLEO*** *glares at* **SLICK***. She motions for her chair.* **SLICK** *struts up to her and gives her an exaggerated bow.)*

SLICK. My dearest Queen. It's been ages.

*(***QUEEN CLEO*** *looks down her nose at* **SLICK***.)*

QUEEN CLEO. Slick…

SLICK. …and you keep getting younger and more beautiful. Why it seems like just yesterday you…

*(***CLEO*** *holds up her hand to cut him off.)*

QUEEN CLEO. Don't waste your razzmatazz on us, Slick. Remember, we know who you are.

SLICK. My Queen, you cut me to the quick. I am your ever faithful servant who…

QUEEN CLEO. Who would steal the fillings out of our teeth. We haven't forgotten about the hummingbirds, Slick. What are you doing in our court, our forest? We banished you.

SLICK. Ah, well, I knew you weren't serious. Just a little irritated at your old friend, Slick. As for the hummingbirds, well, that was a slight misunderstanding, nothing more.

STARE. Who?

CLEO. Humph!

EMMA. There was no…

DONALD. …misunderstanding!

*(***CHEETS*** *rushes over to* **QUEEN** *and tumbles into her knees. He frantically runs around.)*

CHEETS. He's going to take Stanley away from us, Your Majesty! Slick's going to sell Stanley to the circus. Make him dance on the back of a horse, blow fire, sing, dance and be a star. Banish Slick! Banish him!

QUEEN CLEO. CHEETS! Quiet! This is a warning.

(**CHEETS** *immediately sits on the nearest toad stool.* **PERSNICKETY** *crosses to the* **QUEEN**, *takes scissors from her pocket and begins to trim the grass around the* **QUEEN**'s *feet.*)

PERSNICKETY. The grass is far too long here, Your Grace. Your slippers will get damp.

(*The* **QUEEN** *takes* **PERSNICKETY**'s *hand and has her rise.*)

QUEEN CLEO. Thank you but we are certain that the grass can wait. Is there any truth in what Cheets is telling us, Persnickety?

PERSNICKETY. Not if I have anything to say about it. Stanley isn't going *anywhere* without me.

STANLEY. But, Nickety, the circus sounds like a fine place. Mr. Slick says I'll be a star. And you can be my manager, whatever that means.

PERSNICKETY. First of all, stop calling me 'Nickety'. It's babyish and embarrassing. Second of all, *if* Thomas is right and Mr. Slick is a picaroon…

SLICK. Hey!

PERSNICKETY. …and he is the type of person that a queen would banish…Well! He's not for us, Stanley.

STANLEY. But, there's going to be limos, extra towels, fruit!

PERSNICKETY. No.

STANLEY. Gosh, I can't have any fun.

QUEEN CLEO. Slick, for shame. You were encouraging Stanley to run away, *again*, to the circus? Running away from home is a very bad thing to do. You never know who you might meet and what they might do.

(**SLICK** *gives* **CLEO** *an exaggerated bow.*)

SLICK. Another misunderstanding, my Queen. I was just suggesting to Stan that he could better himself, become a star, if he took his many talents to the world of the Big Top.

QUEEN CLEO. Stanley, we will take this under advisement. You are in our forest and therefore you are one of our subjects and under our protection.

STANLEY. Excuse me, your Majesty…Nickety too?

QUEEN CLEO. Of course. You will both stay here until we decide what is best for you.

(**CLEO** *rises. All bow and curtsey.*)

QUEEN CLEO. Emma, Sir Donald. Please look after our guests until we return. Slick?

SLICK. Yes, your Majesty.

QUEEN CLEO. Come with us!

CHEETS. Oh oh!

(*The* **WOODLAND CREATURES** *and* **FAERIES** *all 'oh' and 'ah' thinking* **SLICK** *is in trouble.* **CHEETS** *in a sing-song voice.*)

Slick's gonna get it.…Slick's gonna get it.

Scene Three

(*AT RISE: It is late at night.* **STANLEY** *sleeps on the forest floor on a bed of leaves, snoring occasionally and blowing bubbles with the exhale.* **PERSNICKETY** *is asleep nearby under a blanket of moss.* **SLICK** *sneaks across the stage.* **STARE** *is up in his tree.*)

SLICK. Pssst! (*whispers*) Stanley. (*beat*) Stanley.

(**STANLEY** *rolls over, sits up abruptly.*)

STANLEY. (*in a normal voice.*) What!? What's wrong?

STARE. Who?

SLICK. Shhh! Not so loud. We don't want to wake anyone. It's me, Stan. Your ole' buddy, Slick.

STANLEY. Oh! Hi, Mr. Slick. Is it time to get up?

SLICK. No, no. I just wanted to talk to you. Private, like.

(**STANLEY** *straightens his tie, puts on his glasses.*)

STANLEY. Is it a secret?

SLICK. Naw! But with everybody around, it's hard to think sometimes.

STANLEY. (*holding his head with both hands*) It makes my head hurt.

SLICK. So, let's you and me have a little private meeting, whaddya' say.

STANLEY. Okay. Wait right here, I'll get Persnickety. (*He shouts:*) NICKETY!

SLICK. Shh, shh, shh! No need, my dear boy. Let's just us men talk, how 'bout it?

(*dubious*)

STANLEY. If you think it's okay. But, I'm not supposed to talk to strangers. And if Nickety's going to be my manager shouldn't she be here?

(**SLICK** *laughs.*)

SLICK. 'Strangers'! We're not strangers, Stan. This is your ole' buddy, Slick. Here's the thing, the circus thinks it should manage your career. After all they're the experts. Miss Persnickety is a fine friend but does she have any experience? It's best if she 'keeps the home fires burning'.

STANLEY. Please, Mr. Slick, don't mention 'home fires burning' around Nickety. She's sensitive about it. *(beat)* You mean Nickety isn't coming with us?

SLICK. She'll join you later. Listen, kid are you sure you can't breathe fire? Just a little bit?

STANLEY. I don't think so, Mr. Slick. I've tried before. I've even taken lessons. Nothing works.

SLICK. Well, would you try one more time, for ole' Slick.

STANLEY. Sure.

(**STANLEY** *rears back his head, takes a deep breath and blows…bubbles all over* **SLICK.**)

SLICK. Okay. Okay. *OKAY.* That's enough.

STANLEY. Sorry.

SLICK. Don't worry about it, Kid. We'll take care of the problem when we get to the circus. Just do me a favor, will ya?

STANLEY. Sure. What is it?

SLICK. Don't tell anyone at the circus that you can't breathe fire. I'll tell them at the right moment. Deal?

STANLEY. Well…yeah…but won't they want fire in my act?

SLICK. Yeah, sure but we can worry about that later. Now get your stuff together. We have a long journey and we need to get an early start.

STANLEY. NOW!?

SLICK. Yessiree Bob! 'The early bird gets the worm', I always say.

STANLEY. But, but…

SLICK. Come on now, times awastin'. You want to make your Mom and Dad proud, don'cha?

STANLEY. Yes, but…

SLICK. *(in his best salesmanship manner)* Ya wanna' be a star? Right? The lights, the music, the travel, the fans! All that RAZZMATAZZ!

(**STANLEY** *gets caught up in the excitement.*)

STANLEY. I do! I do!

SLICK. Well, then let's get this show on the road.

(**SLICK** *links arms with* **STANLEY** *and as they exit* **SLICK** *sings the first few stances of the 'Circus Theme Song'.*)

SLICK. Dee, Dee, Dee deedle, deedle, Dee, Dee, Dee….

(They exit.)

Scene Four

(AT RISE: The next morning.)

*(**PERSNICKETY** is pacing back and forth. She is muttering under her breath. All the creatures of the forest watch from the safety of the trees.)*

PERSNICKETY. Oh dear, oh dear, what's to become of us. Where is that bad little dragon? I turn my back for one second and he's gone. Vanished. Poof! Into thin air! How will I ever explain this to his parents. *(She stops and gasps.)* How will I explain this to the *Queen.* Oh dear, oh dear. What shall I do?

*(She runs to **DONALD** and **EMMA** as they enter.)*

Donald! Emma! You must help me!

EMMA. Of course, dear Persnickety…

DONALD. What can we help with?

PERSNICKETY. I must find Stanley.

EMMA. What do you mean?

STARE. Who?

DONALD. Find Stan? He was right here last night.

PERSNICKETY. *He's missing!*

STARE. Who?

EMMA. Not now, Stare.

DONALD. Are you certain? We said good night right here. He was so sleepy he could hardly keep his eyes open.

PERSNICKETY. Well, he's gone now! That bad little dragon.

EMMA. We must find him. We'll help you.

*(**CHEETS** runs on. **THOMAS** plods in after him. **CHEETS** skids to a stop.)*

CHEETS. Hey! *(**CHEETS** is utterly still. He looks around, sniffs the air.)* I don't smell anything. Why don't I smell dragon breath?

*(**PERSNICKETY** rushes to **CHEETS** and **THOMAS**.)*

PERSNICKETY. Oh, Cheets, have you seen Stanley? Or you, Captain Thomas?

CHEETS. Nope. Don't smell him either.

THOMAS. Nothing on the horizon.

STARE. Who?

PERSNICKETY. *(answering* **STARE***)* Stanley. *(beat)* He's gone. Oh no, what shall I do?

THOMAS. Throw me overboard and call me a fish! Pirates are afoot. All hands Hoay!

DONALD. Persnickety, what we must do is call all the woodland creatures and faeries together and launch a thorough search. Stanley can't have gone far.

CHEETS. *(thoughtfully.)* I *should* be able to smell him. After all I have a better nose than any faerie. Bigger feet to run faster…

EMMA. Not now, Cheets.

(All the woodland creatures and faeries begin to emerge from the forest.)

DONALD. Everyone! May I have your attention.

CHEETS. Everyone! Your attention, please!

EMMA. Cheets, please. Let Donald make the announcement.

CHEETS. But I want to. After all, I'm the one who captured him.

EMMA. Cheets, *Please!*

DONALD. I'm going to give you a special assignment, Cheets.

*(***CHEETS*** runs around telling everyone.)*

CHEETS. You hear that? Cheets is getting a special assignment. This elf is very important. Cheets will find Stanley.

DONALD. Now, everyone. Our friend, Stanley, is missing. We must form groups of two or three and search the entire forest. We'll meet back here in two hours. If you find him, bring him back here to our clearing. Thomas, I need you to search the lake.

THOMAS. Aye, Aye, Admiral.

(**THOMAS** *plods off. As he crosses in front of* **STARE**.)

THOMAS. You there, Seaman, hold your position on the poop deck and keep a sharp eye out.

(*All the creatures melt into the forest to search.*)

CHEETS. Donald! Donald! What's my special assignment? Cheets wants to get started immediately.

DONALD. Cheets, you are to see if you can smell dragon's breath. Start from here and work around in larger and larger circles. Use your nose, Cheets, like you've never used it before.

(**CHEETS** *starts from where he stands and makes a tiny circle, sniffing, then continues running in ever increasing circles until he finally disappears into the forest.*)

DONALD. Off you go everyone. Emma and I will search toward her home place.

(*Everyone exits.*)

STARE. (*forlorn*) Whooo?

Intermission

ACT II

Scene One

*(**AT RISE:** The forest. Everyone is returning from the search.)*

DONALD. Any luck? *(beat)* Anyone?

*(Everyone mutters, talking about not finding **STANLEY**. **PERSNICKETY** arrives.)*

PERSNICKETY. Did you find him? Please tell me he has been found.

STARE. Who?

EMMA. No, Nickety, we're sorry. We didn't find him. Donald, we must ask the Queen for help.

*(**CHEETS** bursts onto the stage and screeches to a stop in front of **DONALD**.)*

CHEETS. Nothing! Not a whiff of dragon breath! Nada! I thought I smelled him over by Big Rock, but it was just a skunk. False alarm.

*(**THOMAS** plods in.)*

EMMA. Thomas! Any luck down by the lake?

THOMAS. Nay, Miss Emma. I also checked the bilge, the brig, midships, and the scullery. Nothing. I fear the Swabbie's been deep sixed.

PERSNICKETY. Oh, dear, oh dear. Whatever will I tell Stanley's parents? I promised to keep him safe.

DONALD. I think you're right, Emma. We must send for the Queen.

STARE. Who? Who?

Scene Two

(AT RISE: The next day.)

*(**QUEEN CLEO** sits on her throne with her entourage around her. The **WOODLAND CREATURES** and **FAER-IES** all sit quietly at her feet. **CHEETS** enters at a run. He hurriedly bows to the **QUEEN** and whirls around.)*

CHEETS. Cheets did his best, my Queen. This elf looked and smelled everywhere. Cheets' nose is red and runny from all the smelling that he did. No dragon breath! Not anywhere!

QUEEN CLEO. Thank you, Cheets, for that report. Now, please sit down and be quiet.

CHEETS. Cheets could look again, your Majesty. As soon as my nose gets better Cheets could go on another special assignment.

QUEEN CLEO. Cheets! This is your warning…

*(**CHEETS** continues to run around, tumbling here and there, ignoring the **QUEEN**.)*

CHEETS. Cheets *loves* special assignments! Almost as much as he loves carrots. Your Majesty, Cheets wants…

*(**QUEEN CLEO** snaps her fingers and freezes **CHEETS** into a time out.)*

QUEEN CLEO. Ah. Some silence at last.

*(**DONALD** and **EMMA** enter.)*

Sir Donald. Lady Emma. What news? You asked to see us?

DONALD. Yes, your Majesty, but it's bad news I'm afraid.

EMMA. Stanley is lost again, your Majesty.

STARE. Whooo!?

(All twitter and mutter worried sounds.)

QUEEN CLEO. Are you certain?

EMMA. Yes, my Lady…

DONALD. Yes, your Majesty…

QUEEN CLEO. Is it possible that he simply returned home?

(**PERSNICKETY** *enters. she rushes up to* **DONALD** *and* **EMMA.**)

PERSNICKETY. Have you found him? Please tell me he is safe.

(**DONALD** *and* **EMMA** *shake their heads.*)

QUEEN CLEO. Miss Persnickety, we have just heard about your friend. Is there any chance that he went home?

PERSNICKETY. No, your Majesty. Stanley would not go back without me. *(beat)* Oh, I will do anything to find him. I won't scold him, I won't fuss over him, I won't boss him. He can call me 'Nickety' any time he wants to. Who could have taken him?

STARE. Who? Who? Who?

EMMA. Stare, please. Not now.

(**STARE** *becomes even more agitated. Flapping his wings, fluffing his feathers.*)

STARE. Who! Who! Who!

DONALD. Emma, I think Stare is trying to tell us something. *(beat)* Persnickety, what was it you just said about scolding Stanley?

PERSNICKETY. I was saying that I won't boss him, I promise not to fuss over him…

EMMA. No, after that, Persnickety.

PERSNICKETY. That he could call me 'Nickety'?

DONALD. *(eyeing* **STARE***)* No, something after that.

PERSNICKETY. I don't think I said anything after that…

(**CHEETS** *is squirming to be released from his time out.*)

Oh! Wait! I said…

DONALD. 'who could have taken him'!

PERSNICKETY. Yes.

EMMA. Yes!

(**STARE** *puts his wing tips on his hips trying to imitate* **SLICK***'s mannerisms.*)

STARE. Who! Who! Who!

> (**QUEEN CLEO, DONALD, EMMA,** *and* **PERSNICKETY** *all speak at once.*)

QUEEN CLEO. Slick.

DONALD. Slick.

EMMA. Slick.

PERSNICKETY. Slick!

STARE. *(satisfied)* WHO!

PERSNICKETY. That bad, bad bird! He's taken Stanley.

> (**CHEETS** *is pleading to be released from his time out.*)

QUEEN CLEO. Very well, Cheets. We will release you. But you must behave. We have very serious matters to discuss.

> (*She snaps her fingers.* **CHEETS** *rushes to her.*)

CHEETS. That's what Cheets forgot. Cheets knew there was something he found out on his special assignment. It was what Cheets didn't find.

DONALD. Well, what is it, Cheets.

EMMA. Yes, tell us.

CHEETS. Cheets didn't find Slick! He is nowhere in the forest. *(in hushed tones)* Slick is gone too.

DONALD. He's right, Emma.

EMMA. We haven't seen Slick, that's true. Oh, Donald, how did we miss this important clue?

QUEEN CLEO. Well! Our Mr. City Slick, the third, has much to answer for!

> (**SLICK** *enters. He wears a new bright* **YELLOW** *vest. His derby hat sports a* **YELLOW** *feather. He looks very prosperous. He hums the Circus theme song.*)

SLICK. 'De, de, dettle, dettle'… *(seeing everyone)* Greetings! Did I hear my name mentioned?

> (**SLICK** *makes an elaborate bow to the* **QUEEN.**)

Your Majesty. My dearest Queen. It's been ages and you keep getting younger and more beautiful. Your eyes are like the summer sky, your hair…

QUEEN CLEO. *(a royal command:)* SILENCE! *(beat)* We are most unhappy with you, Slick.

(**SLICK** *is all innocence.*)

SLICK. But, my fairest of ladies, why?

QUEEN CLEO. What do you know about our friend, Stanley the Stalwart, disappearing?

SLICK. What? My friend, my ole' buddy, has run away *again?*

DONALD. No one said anything about Stanley running away, Slick.

SLICK. Okay, disappeared then. What's the difference?

EMMA. Please, Mr. Slick, if you know anything, please tell us where to find him.

SLICK. Sorry, Missy, I would if I could. I've been back to town. Don't know anything about Stan disappearing.

DONALD. You're fibbing, Slick. That's all you talked about to Stanley. The circus this, the circus that.

PERSNICKETY. Oh no! You didn't take him to the circus. Tell me you didn't. Stanley will be so frightened.

SLICK. Whatever do you mean, little Lady? I didn't do anything. Sure, I told Stan how much fun a circus is but I never meant anything by it. *(innocence)* You don't think he ran away to the circus, do you?

(**CHEETS** *runs circles around* **SLICK** *and in a sing-song voice.*)

CHEETS. City Slick's a fibber. Pants on fire! City Slick's a fibber.

QUEEN CLEO. Slick?

STARE. *(accusingly)* WHO!

SLICK. Your Majesty. Your most gracious Monarch. I am at your service.

QUEEN CLEO. What do you know about Stanley's whereabouts?

(**CHEETS** *begins to sniff around* **SLICK.** *He gets closer and closer, sniffing.* **SLICK** *tries to move away.*)

SLICK. Hey! What are you doing!? Get away from me.

CHEETS. I smell…

(**CHEETS** *gets closer.*)

SLICK. Get off me. Get away, I say!

CHEETS. I smell…

(**CHEETS** *sniffs harder.*)

SLICK. You don't smell anything! Get off!

CHEETS. I smell DRAGON BREATH! *(beat)* And cotton candy!

DONALD. Cheets, are you certain?

EMMA. Oh, Slick….

SLICK. No you don't. It must be my new cologne.

QUEEN CLEO. This is a most serious accusation, Cheets. It is not a time for playing and frolicking around. Do you swear that you smell Stanley and the circus on Slick?

CHEETS. I am positive, your Grace. There is a whiff of dragon breath with an underpinning of cotton candy. If I am lying I'll never eat another carrot in my life time. Everyone knows how much Cheets loves his carrots.

QUEEN CLEO. Very well. We believe you. *(beat)* Slick! Approach us.

SLICK. *(Dragging his feet, he crosses to the **QUEEN**.)* My Queen?

QUEEN CLEO. Can you deny that you had something to do with Stanley the Stalwart, disappearing?

SLICK. *(denying yet again)* Your most exquisite Majesty, I know nothing…

QUEEN CLEO. Beware, Slick. Be very cautious with your answer. If you tell a lie and we catch you, you will be banished for all time. Banished from this forest, from the city lights you love so much, banished from this planet. You know that we can do this so think about your answer very carefully.

ALL. Banish him! Banish him!

QUEEN CLEO. Silence. Well, Slick what do you have to say to us?

SLICK. Well, I might have had a little something to do with Stan looking to improve his life. He really wanted to be a star, your Majesty.

PERSNICKETY. Oh no!

DONALD. I knew it.

EMMA. How could you?

(**CHEETS** *runs around.*)

CHEETS. Didn't Cheets say? Cheets' nose smelled dragon breath. Cotton candy too! Slick is a bad, bad, bird. Banish him!

(*The* **QUEEN** *gives* **CHEETS** *a look and he immediately sits down.*)

CHEETS. See how quiet this elf can be?

QUEEN CLEO. (*commanding*) Tell us everything, Slick.

SLICK. Well, a few nights ago, Stan came to me and said he really, *really* wanted to see the circus. He said if he became a star his folks would be so proud of him and then he could go back home in style. He pleaded with me to take him to the next town where the circus would be…

(*The* **QUEEN** *is not believing any of it.*)

QUEEN CLEO. How much did you get for him, Slick?

SLICK. Your Majesty, you wound me.

QUEEN CLEO. How much?

SLICK. Two hundred dollars.

QUEEN CLEO. Give us the money.

SLICK. I don't have all of it. You see I have expenses, entertainments, hotels, cab fare, tips…

QUEEN CLEO. Enough! How much do you have left?

(**SLICK** *takes out a wad of money and counts. He puts a bill back in his pocket.*)

SLICK. One hundred-forty dollars and some change, your Majesty.

QUEEN CLEO. Give it to Donald.

SLICK. But, your Majesty, I...I...

QUEEN CLEO. *(commanding)* Now.

> *(SLICK crosses to DONALD and hands over the money.)*

QUEEN CLEO. All of it!

> *(SLICK sighs and digs into his pocket for the other ten and gives it to DONALD.)*

QUEEN CLEO. We must find Stanley the Stalwart, and buy him back from the circus.

> *(Everyone cheers.)*

DONALD. But, Queen Cleo, we don't have the whole amount. Will the circus take less for Stanley than what they paid?

EMMA. I have ten dollars at home. You can have that.

DONALD. I still have the gold piece you gave me last year, your Majesty. That's worth maybe fourteen dollars?

> *(CHEETS takes his hat and passes it around the WOODLAND CREATURES and other FAERIES. All drop in coins. He quickly counts it.)*

CHEETS. We've collected six dollars, Donald.

PERSNICKETY. Stanley and I had some emergency traveling funds. Here's five more, Donald.

DONALD. We're fifteen dollars short.

STARE. Who?

EMMA. Oh dear.

QUEEN CLEO. Not to worry, dear Emma. *(She addresses one of her ladies.)* Scarlet, our reticule if you please.

> *(SCARLET hands the QUEEN a velvet purse. she removes some gold coins.)*

Sir Donald, Lady Emma, please kneel before us.

> *(DONALD and EMMA cross to her and kneel.)*

EMMA. Yes, your Majesty.

DONALD. Your Grace.

QUEEN CLEO. We have a new quest for you both. If you decide to accept it you will be guided by Slick to the town where…

SLICK. But, your Majesty, I am expected in the city…

QUEEN CLEO. Silence! You are responsible for Stanley running away. If you hadn't painted a glamorous picture of bright lights and cotton candy Stanley the Stalwart would still be safe and here with us in our forest.

(She turns back to **EMMA** *and* **DONALD**.*)*

Slick shall guide you to the town where Stanley was last seen. You shall attempt to give the money back to the owners of the circus in exchange for Stanley's freedom. With all haste you shall return to our forest. Sir Donald, Lady Emma? Do you accept this quest.

*(***DONALD*** *and* ***EMMA*** *bow their heads.)*

DONALD. Yes, my Lady.

EMMA. Yes, you Majesty.

QUEEN CLEO. You are our true and loyal subjects. We expected no less of you. *(beat)* Emma, dear, you must ask your mother's permission before you start out. Is that understood?

EMMA. Yes, my Queen.

(The **QUEEN** *hands* **DONALD** *the gold coins.)*

QUEEN CLEO. You shall leave tomorrow at first light. *(beat)* Slick, we expect to find you still here in the morning. Is that clear?

(hangs his head)

SLICK. Yes, your Grace.

PERSNICKETY. If it pleases your Majesty, I would like to go with Donald and Emma. After all, Stanley is my best friend and my responsibility.

QUEEN CLEO. Of course, dear Lady. We never meant for you not to go. *(Beat. The* **QUEEN** *rises to exit.)* Tomorrow, then.

Scene Three

(AT RISE: A few hours later. Set change. The main tent of the Circus. Circus music.)

(FRECKLES, the owner and ring master, stands on a large drum in the center ring of the circus. The audience is clapping and cheering.)

FRECKLES. LADIES and GENTLEMEN! CHILDREN OF ALL AGES! Sit back in your seats, hang onto your hats, and prepare to see, for the first time anywhere in the world, a terrifying, fire breathing DRAGON! Captured in the far jungles of Borneo and brought here for your enjoyment! Now, in the center ring, the ninth wonder of the world, Zindarth, the fire breathing dragon.

(Accompanied by music, small clowns, a ballerina and other circus folk, STANLEY is led into the ring by a chain on his leg. STANLEY wears a Tutu and a crown with feather plumes. He looks ridiculous. He is led to the center of the ring. FRECKLES addresses the audience.)

FRECKLES. Don't get any closer, my friends. This fierce dragon can singe the hair off your head, can curl the toes of your shoes, can give you a sun burn with just one breath! ARE YOU READY!?

(soundt of the audience going wild)

Maestro, drum roll, if you please. The Dragon will now BREATHE FIRE!!!

(Drum roll. STANLEY takes a deep inhale, rears back his head and blows bubbles all over the circus folk, FRECKLES, and the audience. At first, the audience laughs; then realize there will be no fire. They begin to boo and hiss. STANLEY is led off in shame.)

FRECKLES. Not to worry, dear friends, our fearsome dragon seems to have caught a cold. Please stay in your seats for more excitement. Bare back riders, lions, tigers, elephants, the man on the flying trapeze, and much, much more!

Scene Four

*(AT **RISE RISE**: Backstage at the circus. **STANLEY** lies on some dirty old canvas on the tent floor.)*

*(**STANLEY** is forlorn. He sighs and bubbles erupt. He moves his leg. He is chained.)*

STANLEY. Oh my. What have I done? I should never, never have run away.

*(Eerily, the ballerina, in toe shoes, pirouettes across the stage and is gone. **FRECKLES** enters.)*

FRECKLES. Well, Stanley? Any fire yet?

STANLEY. No Sir, Mr. Freckles.

FRECKLES. Have you been trying?

STANLEY. Yes, sir.

FRECKLES. What a bust! I can't present you as the ninth wonder of the world without FIRE, man! You must try harder.

STANLEY. I have, Sir. For years now. I told Mr. Slick that I didn't have any fire in me.

FRECKLES. What!?

STANLEY. Mr. Slick. He knew. Didn't he tell you? He promised that he would tell you 'when the moment was right.'

FRECKLES. *(pounding his fist in his own hand)* SLICK! I should have known. He's not called 'Slick' for nuthin'!

*(**STANLEY** sighs and blows bubbles.)*

FRECKLES. And you! Stop blowing those bubbles all over the circus tent.

STANLEY. Sorry, Sir.

FRECKLES. You will stay here until you give me some fire! I'm out a lotta' money because of you. Not only the cash I gave to that scoundrel, but also for your upkeep. Good grief, I never knew a dragon could eat so much!

*(**FRECKLES** stomps off.)*

STANLEY. I am such a disappointment to everyone. I wish
Nickety was here. And my new friends from the forest.
(He lays his head back down.) I want to go home.

(The ballerina silently pirouettes back across the stage.)

Scene Five

(AT RISE: Outside the circus tent **EMMA** *enters.* **FRECKLES** *is putting the final touches on his costume.)*

*(***EMMA*** *crosses to* **FRECKLES***.)*

EMMA. Excuse me, Mr. Freckles?

FRECKLES. Hey! Kids can't come back stage. Go back out front with your folks, little girl.

EMMA. No, Sir, I didn't come to see the show. *(realizes that might sound rude)* I'm certain that it's a wonderful show. But, I've come on a very important mission.

FRECKLES. Yeah? What's so important, little missy.

EMMA. My name is Emma. And I believe that my friend, Stanley the Stalwart is here with you.

FRECKLES. What makes you think that?

EMMA. Our mutual acquaintance, Mr. Slick, told me so.

FRECKLES. Slick again!

EMMA. Yes, and I've come to return your money and to take Stanley home.

FRECKLES. You have, have you?

EMMA. Yes sir. *(She pats her pocket.)* I have all your money right here. If you could just tell me where you are keeping Stanley, I'll...

FRECKLES. Ha! I don't want your money! As soon as that dragon starts to blow...

EMMA. So! You do have him!

FRECKLES. Yeah, so what? I paid for him fair and square.

EMMA. But I can give you a complete refund and then take him home.

FRECKLES. Not so fast there little Miss. I've got a lot invested in that dragon. As soon as he gets some fire built up I'm gonna be a rich man. Why if he only does two shows a day my fortune is made.

EMMA. But, Mr. Freckles, he can't breathe fire. Didn't he tell you?

FRECKLES. Yeah, that's what he said. But, we all know that dragons breathe fire. *That's what they do!*

EMMA. Not Stanley. He's gentle and kind. He doesn't want to set anything on fire. If Mr. Slick told you he could, well then,…he told you a lie.

FRECKLES. Listen you! That dragon will breathe fire or my name isn't Freckles the Clown. Now get outta here, kid and no more nonsense. Go on! Shoo!

Scene Six

(AT RISE: Night. The circus, backstage.)

(STANLEY lays on the ground. A 'barn boy' enters with a pail in each hand. He wears a cap pulled down low over his ears. He looks around to make certain that no one is about.)

DONALD. *(whispering)* Pssst. Stanley.

(STANLEY doesn't hear. DONALD whispers louder.)

DONALD. Stanley!

(STANLEY burps a couple of bubbles but doesn't respond.)

DONALD. *Dragon Breath!* Wake up!

(STANLEY sits up.)

STANLEY. Huh?

DONALD. Stan! It's me, Donald.

STANLEY. Donald? Oh, Donald is it really you? Am I glad to see you! How did you find me?

DONALD. Never mind that now. How're you doing, Stan? Are you okay?

STANLEY. Can I go home now, Donald? I don't like the circus. Mr. Slick brought me here and he didn't tell Mr. Freckles that I can't breathe fire. Mr. Freckles is very disappointed in me and now I have to wear this chain and every time I try to breathe fire I blow bubbles all over Mr. Freckles' tent. That really makes him mad. *(beat)* I wanna go home.

DONALD. Take it easy, Stan. Emma and Persnickety and I came to get you. Emma is giving Mr. Freckles his money back right now.

STANLEY. Nickety? She's here? Nickety's here!

DONALD. Yes. Now that I see that the coast is clear… *(He motions with his hand.)* Persnickety!

(PERSNICKETY runs to STANLEY.)

PERSNICKETY. Stanley, at last we have found you. How are you, dear friend?

STANLEY. I want to go home, Nickety.

> (**PERSNICKETY** *looks around* **STANLEY** *in horror at the mess. Begins to sweep, and clean up.*)

PERSNICKETY. Yes, yes, of course you do. And we're all going home together. Emma and Donald are helping me. What a pig sty. How can anyone live like this.

STANLEY. I want to go home RIGHT NOW!

PERSNICKETY. Soon. Now let's get you presentable. (*fusses over him*) Let me straighten your tie, Stanley.

> (**EMMA** *enters.*)

DONALD. Emma, over here.

STANLEY. Hello, Emma.

DONALD. Emma, did you see Mr. Freckles? Did you give him the money?

EMMA. We have a big, big problem, Donald. Mr. Freckles wouldn't take his money back and he doesn't want to give Stanley to us.

PERSNICKETY. Oh dear, whatever are we to do? Look Emma, That bad clown has chained my darling dragon's leg.

STANLEY. I want to go home.

DONALD. But why, Emma? Stanley's no good to him without the fire.

EMMA. Mr. Freckles believes that Stanley will eventually breathe fire.

STANLEY. I can't. I don't want to.

PERSNICKETY. No, of course you don't.

> (**DONALD** *and* **EMMA** *move away.*)

DONALD. What should we do, Emma?

EMMA. Our quest is to save Stanley. The Queen expects us to succeed. We must launch a daring rescue. Tomorrow night.

DONALD. Why not tonight?

EMMA. Mr. Freckles might be on the alert. He thinks that I went home since he turned me down but we can't take a chance. Besides, we need a day to make our new plans.

(They cross back to **STANLEY** *and* **PERSNICKETY**.*)*

PERSNICKETY. What are we to do?

DONALD. We are going to launch a daring rescue.

EMMA. Stanley, do they keep this chain on your leg at all times?

STANLEY. Yes, Miss Emma. *(beat)* When can I go home?

EMMA. Soon, my friend, very soon. We need to find a way to get this chain off. Stanley, is there a key?

STANLEY. Yes.

DONALD. Great! Where is it?

STANLEY. Mr. Freckles wears it on a chain that is hooked to his belt.

EMMA. Well, then a key is out. Donald, what can we do without the key?

DONALD. All circuses have work shops. I'll find it *and* a tool strong enough to cut the chain off.

PERSNICKETY. Good idea. Now, Stanley it's very important that you act normally if Mr. Freckles comes by. You can't tell *anyone* that we are here.

EMMA. We'll all meet back here tomorrow night after the circus people have gone to sleep. While Donald finds a tool in the work shop, I will find the fastest and safest way out of here. Persnickety will stay here and protect Stanley. Agreed?

*(***DONALD** *and* **EMMA** *exit.)*

STANLEY. Nickety, I'm sorry I left without you. I made a big fat mistake, running away to join the circus. Don't leave me.

PERSNICKETY. I won't. I'll be right here. After all, who's going to notice a Lady Bug? Try to get some sleep now.

*(***FRECKLES** *enters. He does not see a lady bug flitting around.)*

FRECKLES. Anything yet, Stanley? Smoke? Fire?

STANLEY. No sir. Would you like me to try again?

FRECKLES. Not if you are going to breathe bubbles all over everything.

STANLEY. Then does that mean I can go home with…

(**PERSNICKETY** *runs over to* **STANLEY** *and pokes him in the back. Whispers.*)

PERSNICKETY. Stanley! No!

(**STANLEY** *burbs a bubble or two.*)

STANLEY. Huh?

FRECKLES. Huh?

STANLEY. Nothing, Sir. I just burped on a bubble. Excuse me.

FRECKLES. Well, keep trying. You're not leaving this tent until you give me some fire. (*grumbles as he exits*) I can't believe how much this is costing me…if I ever see that City Slick again, he'll be sorry. Whoever heard of a dragon that can't breathe fire!

PERSNICKETY. Whew! That was close. Stanley, you mustn't say anything about me or Donald and Emma. Do you understand how important that is?

(**STANLEY** *hangs his head.*)

STANLEY. I'm sorry. (*beat*) You're not going to leave me, are you Nickety?

PERSNICKETY. No, I'll be right here with you until Donald and Emma return.

STANLEY. I want to go home.

PERSNICKETY. I know, Stanley, I know.

Scene Seven

(AT RISE: The next night. Circus music fades into the night. All is silent.)

*(**EMMA** and **DONALD** sneak into the tent. **DONALD** carries a large tool and safety glasses. **PERSNICKETY** motions them over. **STANLEY** is snoring.)*

PERSNICKETY. Is everyone asleep?

DONALD. It seems so.

EMMA. All's quiet.

STANLEY. *(wakes up)* Huh? Is it time to go home now?

PERSNICKETY. Shh! Stanley, keep your voice down.

STANLEY. Why?

EMMA. Because it's a big secret, remember? We're rescuing you so you can go home. Donald, let's see if the tool will cut the chain off.

PERSNICKETY. Keep your leg very still, Stanley.

STANLEY. Okay. But, Donald, aren't you suppose to have a grown-up here if you work with tools that big?

*(**DONALD** puts on the safety glasses and grins at **STANLEY**.)*

DONALD. It's okay, buddy. My father taught me how to be safe. You should always wear safety glasses and be very careful when you use tools.

STANLEY. Glasses like mine?

DONALD. Not exactly…

*(As **DONALD** begins to work on the chain, noise and footsteps are heard off.)*

EMMA. *(whispers)* Someone's coming! Quick, hide!

*(**DONALD** and **EMMA** run and hide behind the large drum, leaving the tool behind in plain sight. **PERSNICKETY** stays close to **STANLEY**. She sees the tool.)*

PERSNICKETY. Donald! The tool!

*(**DONALD** dashes back out and grabs the tool and hides again. **FRECKLES** enters.)*

STANLEY. H…H…Hello, Mr. Freckles.

FRECKLES. Stanley. Just dropped by to check on you before I go to bed. Any fire yet? Puffs of smoke? Anything?

STANLEY. No, sir.

FRECKLES. Very unusual indeed. Tell me, did your parents breathe fire?

STANLEY. Oh, yes! My father is a famous fire breathing dragon. He's one of the best!

FRECKLES. Too bad Slick didn't have *him* for sale. What's your father say about a son who can only breathe bubbles?

STANLEY. He's very disappointed in me, sir.

FRECKLES. No more than I, Stan, no more than I.

(FRECKLES exits. All is quiet. DONALD and EMMA's heads peek over the drum. They whisper.)

DONALD. Wow, that was close!

EMMA. Is he gone?

PERSNICKETY. Shh! Let me follow him and be certain.

(PERSNICKETY flies off and returns almost immediately.)

I followed him to his wagon. He's turned out his lights and gone to bed.

DONALD. Good. Let's get back to work. Emma, please hold Stan's foot while I cut the chain.

(They set to work. STANLEY begins to giggle and burp bubbles.)

EMMA. Stanley, hush!

STANLEY. That tickles. My feet are so ticklish. *(He continues to giggle louder.)*

PERSNICKETY. Do be quiet.

DONALD. Stan, shush, someone will hear you.

STANLEY. But it tickles.

(There is a loud clunk as the chain breaks.)

DONALD. Got it! The chain is off!

EMMA. Good work, Donald.

PERSNICKETY. Free at last.

STANLEY. Can we go home now?

EMMA. Yes, Stanley, *now* we can all go home.

DONALD. Emma, I think you should go first and signal us when it's safe. Stanley and Persnickety will go next and I will bring up the rear.

   (**EMMA** *notices she still has the money in her pocket.*)

EMMA. That sounds good, Donald. Oh, dear. I still have Mr. Freckles' money.

PERSNICKETY. What should we do with it?

EMMA. I know. We'll put it here, (*She puts the money under the tool and chain.*) under the tool and chain. Maybe Mr. Freckles will get the message that it is not nice to buy *anyone* and keep them locked up.

DONALD. Good idea. Now, we should leave by the far side of the tent, away from Mr. Freckles and his wagon.

   (*They all creep across the tent and* **EMMA** *exits first. Seconds later,* **EMMA** *pops her head back in.*)

EMMA. Hurry, everyone. The coast is clear.

STANLEY. Am I going home now, Nickety?

   (**PERSNICKETY** *picks lint off* **STANLEY** *and straightens his tie.*)

PERSNICKETY. Yes, Stanley we are finally going home.

   (**STANLEY** *and* **PERSNICKETY** *exit.* **DONALD** *waits and turns to be certain that no one has entered the tent. He exits.*)

Scene Eight

(AT RISE: Set change. The forest is filled with music and laughter.)

(QUEEN CLEO is sitting on her throne. Her LADIES are around her. All the woodland creatures and the faeries are there. STARE is in his tree. CHEETS rushes on.)

CHEETS. They're coming! They're coming! They've got *Dragon Breath* with them!

(Everyone cheers.)

STARE. Who?

CHEETS. Didn't Cheets say? This elf knew Emma and Donald would fulfill their quest.

(Everyone cheers as DONALD, EMMA, STANLEY and PERSNICKETY enter. EMMA and STANLEY are wearing crowns of flowers. They cross to the QUEEN; DONALD bows deeply, EMMA and PERSNICKETY curtsey. PER-SNICKETY pokes STANLEY and he bows deeply too.)

QUEEN CLEO. Lady Emma, Sir Donald. You have done well.

EMMA. Thank you, your Majesty.

DONALD. Thank you, your Grace.

QUEEN CLEO. Tell us of your journey.

(CHEETS runs around, tumbling into everyone.)

CHEETS. A story! Cheets wants to hear a story! Cheets could have saved Stanley. This elf is very brave. Tell us, tell us!

QUEEN CLEO. Cheets! Do you want a time out?

CHEETS. No! Cheets wants a story.

QUEEN CLEO. Then everyone sit down quietly. That means you too, Cheets.

(CHEETS abruptly sits on a toad stool. Everyone sits.)

EMMA. Donald, you start.

DONALD. Your Majesty, if it pleases you. After Slick showed us where the circus was we stayed out of sight and made our plans. First, Emma went to see the owner, Mr. Freckles, and I disguised myself as a barn boy…

STARE. Who?

DONALD. A barn boy. He carries feed and fresh water to the animals.

CHEETS. Cheets would make an excellent 'barn boy'.

QUEEN CLEO. Please continue Donald.

DONALD. I went to the tent where Stanley was being kept. They had Stanley chained up.

(Everyone groans.)

QUEEN CLEO. That's terrible.

SCARLET. How could they?

GREEN. Stanley was a slave?

PERSNICKETY. Yes! It was awful!

DONALD. Tell them about Mr. Freckles, Emma.

STARE. Who?

CHEETS. Was he scary? I bet he was. Did he have bad teeth, warts, scaly skin, hair on his hands, was he smelly?

QUEEN CLEO. Cheets.

*(**CHEETS** quiets.)*

EMMA. No, Cheets, he was a sad clown. Mr. Freckles was in his tent getting ready for the show. I introduced myself and explained that there had been a misunderstanding and that I had brought his money back to him. And would he please give Stanley to me. But, he refused. He sent me away.

CHEETS. *Plan B!*

DONALD. Yes, we had to go to plan 'B'. Persnickety stayed with Stan while Emma and I put our plans into place.

CHEETS. I should have been there. Cheets in a good planner…bigger brain…

DONALD. *(interrupting)* We had to get the chain off Stan's leg and there was no key. I found the work shop at the circus and a tool that I thought would cut the chain.

(Everyone cheers and claps.)

DONALD. *(cont.)* The next night, when the circus was asleep, we crept into Stanley's tent and began working on the chain.

QUEEN CLEO. Did you wear safety glasses, Donald?

DONALD. Yes, Ma-am.

STANLEY. But, then Mr. Freckles came and almost caught us. Donald and Emma were very brave.

CHEETS. This elf is the bravest. Cheets would have *chewed* the chain off. Bigger teeth…

QUEEN CLEO. Cheets…What happened next?

PERSNICKETY. They hid until Mr. Freckles left. I stayed with Stanley. Then Donald worked and worked and finally got the chain off. Then we all escaped.

(Everyone cheers.)

QUEEN CLEO. Well done, Emma. Excellent, Donald. Well done by all!

EMMA. Your Majesty, may I ask what happened to Mr. Slick?

(CHEETS *jumps up.)*

CHEETS. I know, I know! Slick was banished!

QUEEN CLEO. I am afraid Cheets is correct, Emma. Slick had to be punished for endangering our friend and then lying to us. He is banished from this forest and the city lights and our presence for one year.

ALL. Oooooo.

QUEEN CLEO. Now to happier subjects. Stanley and Persnickety please approach us. Kneel.

(STANLEY *and* **PERSNICKETY** *kneel in front of the* **QUEEN.** *)*

QUEEN CLEO. Nickety, my dear, we make you a Lady of our court. Whenever you are at court you shall attend us. Here is a token of our affection.

(QUEEN CLEO *gives* **PERSNICKETY** *a golden dust pan.)*

PERSNICKETY. Oh! Thank you, your Majesty.

QUEEN CLEO. Rise Lady Persnickety.

(**PERSNICKETY** *rises and moves to the side with the other handmaidens.*)

QUEEN CLEO. Now! For our friendly dragon.

(**STANLEY** *hangs his head. He believes he is in trouble.*)

STANLEY. Yes, your Majesty. I know I was a bad dragon running away ...

(*The* **QUEEN** *silences him.*)

QUEEN CLEO. (*smiling fondly*) Stanley, you have made some bad decisions. First running away from home and then running away *again* to the circus. Dreadful things could have happened to you not only at the circus but when you were lost in our forest. But that is how we learn in life, making mistakes and learning from them. You are kind and gentle. You have no wish to burn and destroy things by breathing fire. You are a good friend, Stanley the Stalwart. We would hope that you have learned that you are very special even if you can't breathe fire. People love you because you *are* so unique.

(*The* **QUEEN** *lays her scepter on* **STANLEY***'s shoulder.*)

Therefore, we wish to make you a knight of our court. We dub you, Sir Stanley, the Stalwart! Rise, Sir Stanley.

(*Everyone cheers.*)

What can we give you, Sir Stanley?

STANLEY. I want to go home, your Majesty.

QUEEN CLEO. Then you shall. We will help you. However, remember, Lady Persnickety and Sir Stanley the Stalwart will always be welcome here in our forest.

Scene Nine

(AT RISE: Early morning. Everyone from the forest, including **EMMA,** *the* **QUEEN, CHEETS, THOMAS, DONALD** *are gathered around* **STANLEY** *and* **PERSNICKETY** *to see them on their way.)*

STANLEY. Do you have the compass, Nickety?

*(***PERSNICKETY** *has a small canvas bag in her arms.)*

PERSNICKETY. Yes, and the map. We're ready to go.

THOMAS. A good seaman would use the stars to chart his way.

*(***EMMA** *steps forward and hugs first* **PERSNICKETY** *and then* **STANLEY.***)*

EMMA. Don't forget us. Come back and see us.

*(***STANLEY** *rubs his eyes.)*

STANLEY. We won't forget, Miss Emma.

(Handing **STANLEY** *a hanky.)*

PERSNICKETY. Don't cry Stanley, you'll fog up your glasses.

*(***STANLEY** *and* **PERSNICKETY** *cross to the far side of the stage.* **STANLEY** *gets a running start across the stage and "flies away." Exit. Everyone begins to cheer and wave. Their cheering and waving dies as they realize that* **STANLEY** *is going in the wrong direction.)*

EMMA. Oh no! Donald, Stanley is going the wrong way!

STARE. Who?

EMMA. Stanley.

*(***EMMA** *and* **DONALD** *begin yelling at* **STANLEY** *and waving their arms.* **CHEETS** *joins in.)*

DONALD. Stan! You're going the wrong direction!

EMMA. Persnickety, look at the compass!

*(***CHEETS** *runs around, yelling.)*

CHEETS. Dragon breath has no sense of direction! No wonder he's always lost.

*(***CHEETS** *stumbles and immediately turns it into a sum-mersault.)*

CHEETS. Dragon Breath, turn around!

EMMA. Look! Persnickety is using the compass. She is jumping up and down and pointing north.

*(Another cheer goes up as ***STANLEY*** makes a slow turn in the sky and flies in the correct direction. Everyone watches and turns as ***STANLEY*** makes the turn. He and ***PERSNICKETY*** fly out of sight.)*

THOMAS. By all that swims under the sea, that's no sea monster. Stan can fly!

EMMA. I am so happy that this ended well, Donald. But I will miss our new friends so very much. *(beat)* Running away from home is always a bad idea.

DONALD. I agree, Emma. You can't run away from your problems.

EMMA. You have to stay and face them. Talk to your parents. That's the way to truly solve problems. My mother has always said that no matter what I can tell her anything.

STARE. Who?

CHEETS. Cheets doesn't have any problems!

THOMAS. Being's that I'm the Captain, I must solve everyone's problems!

DONALD. I can tell my Dad anything and I know that he will help me even if what I have done is wrong.

EMMA. And if my mother wasn't around, I could always talk to my best friend.

DONALD. Oh? And who would that be?

EMMA. Why, you, of course!

STARE. Who?

(curtain)

GLOSSARY

"Motley crew", refers to inferior, varied, mixed.

"Batten down the hatches" Close all the windows and doors.

"Hesperides" pronounced: hes per' i dez

"What can I do you for?" is not a grammatical error.

"Burbs" Slick refers to the forest as the 'burbs'; as in suburbs

"Rubes" are the marks, the suckers, for con-men.

"Topsail" is pronounced: 'top-saul'

"Rag" refers to sails.

"Swabbie" refers to a sailor or deck hand

"Freebooters" are pirates

"Aft" is to the rear of the boat

"Starboard" is to the right.

"Stow" is to put away, storage.

"Grog" is a rum drink sailors received.

"Mizzen mast" is the mast located to the rear [aft] of the 'main mast'

Ladies aboard Thomas' ships. Historically it was considered 'bad luck' for ships to have women aboard and they were rarely allowed.

"Hold" the storage below the decks.

"Squall" is a storm

"Picaroon" Spanish for 'rascal'

"Davy Jones' Locker" the bottom of the sea.

"Boatswain" is deck crew

"Reef the sails" Reduce or Shorten the sail when there is too much wind.

"Hornswoggle" is to fool or cheat someone.

"Nickety" is Stanley's nickname for Persnickety.

"Landlubbers" are people who are more comfortable on land and know very little about the sea.

"We" the Queen speaks with the royal "we" at all times. Never "I".

"All hands Hoay" Calling all hands on Deck for action; work or fighting pirates.

"Poop Deck" is the highest deck on a ship.

"Bilge" space below the hold. Usually full of brackish sea water.

"Brig" Military jail

"Midships" middle of boat

"Scullery" kitchen

"Deep six" over board

"Reticule" a lady's small purse

**Also by
Trisha Sugarek…**

Emma and the Lost Unicorn

The Guyer Girls

**The Exciting Exploits of
an Effervescent Elf**

OTHER TITLES AVAILABLE FROM SAMUEL FRENCH

EMMA AND THE LOST UNICORN

Trisha Sugarek

*Fantasy / 4m, 5f, 6 additional speaking roles & additional
non-speaking roles / Single Set*

Rainey, the unicorn, is a prince who has been banished to the forest
for centuries by the warlock, Kodak. The prince can never return
home unless someone solves more riddles than the warlock and
discovers Kodak's secret weakness. A surprise twist ending makes
this modern fable appealing to adults and children alike. Mythical
creatures, scary henchmen, a warlock, queen, faeries, all co-habit
an enchanted forest with giggles provided by a rhetorical owl and
a naughty elf.

www.ingramcontent.com/pod-product-compliance
Lightning Source LLC
Chambersburg PA
CBHW070406120726
47909CB00005B/1656